In Juliet's Garden

A Comedy in One Act

by Judy Elliot McDonald

FOUNDED 1830

SAMUELFRENCH.COM

CHARACTERS

NURSE – Juliet's Nurse. She is also the Widow from *Taming of the Shrew*, and Mistress Quickly from *Henry IV Part 1*. Sweet and kindly.

PORTIA – (*Merchant of Venice*) imperious and self-controlled

KATHARINA – (*Taming of the Shrew*) rough and ready

JULIET – (*Romeo and Juliet*) sweet but spoiled

OPHELIA – (*Hamlet*) a basket case

DESDEMONA – (*Othello*) always a little confused

JACQUELINE DE BOYS – name borrowed from Jacque de Boys from *As You Like It*. Shakespeare's editor and literary agent. Has met all the ladies before and has some definite opinions about each one.

(Optional ending: **WILLIAM SHAKESPEARE** – traditionally dressed)

SETTING

A garden of the Capulet estate, Verona, anytime.

PRODUCTION HISTORY

IN JULIET'S GARDEN was first performed by the Waterfront
Players Repertory Company in North Bend, Oregon in 2000 as a
twenty-minute short. In 2002 ***IN JULIET'S GARDEN*** was awarded
production in this format at the Festival of Inspired Shakespeare
Shorts in Calgary, Alberta, Canada, performed by the Festival
Company. In 2003, a thirty-minute version of the play and won the
2003 Oregon AACT/Fest for the Waterfront Players in McMin-
nville, Oregon.

In 2006, the final version, as a fifty-minute one-act, the play was
produced by the Waterfront Players Repertory Company, North
Bend, Oregon. The production was directed by Judy McDonald,
the Technical Direction by Pat McDonald, the Light and Sound
operator was Nolan Hofferber with the following cast:

PORTIA . . . . Carolyn Agee
KATHARINA . . . . Rosalia D'Amato
OPHELIA . . . . Wavey Shaver
DESDEMONA . . . . Hilary Clayton
JULIET'S NURSE . . . . Judy McDonald
JULIET . . . . Aubrae Hathaway
JACQUELINE DE BOYS . . . . Marla Taylor

SPECIAL THANKS

The author wishes to thank Josiah Phillips, Pat McDonald and Lowell Kobrin for their contributions to this final version of In Juliet's Garden.

(Lights up. Birdsong. **PORTIA** *is pre-set in audience. She is dressed in very severe contemporary business attire, with briefcase. Cell phone rings and she looks in her purse.)*

PORTIA. Oh, why can't I ever find that phone? *(Finds phone.)* Hello Nerissa, just a moment, *(to surrounding irate audience members)* excuse me, so sorry, pardon me *(as she exits row)* good you got my text message. *(Again to nearby audience)* Sorry, I really must take this. Nerissa, could you please double-check Juliet's address for me, please? I don't seem to be able to locate the house.

(Enter **KATHARINA**. *She is dressed in traditional Shakespearean garb, but a little loud).*

KATHARINA. Portia *(interrupting phone conversation)* is that you?

PORTIA. OK, I've got it. Yes, this looks like it. Thanks Nerissa, yes that's all. Goodbye.

KATHARINA. It is, isn't it? Well, I haven't seen you since we were double billed in Ontario a few seasons ago. *(Notices her suit and brief case)* Interesting costume concept. Who's the designer?

PORTIA. *(Coolly)* Yes, a *very* modern production at Center Stage in Baltimore. Can't remember the designer's name. Certainly works for the role, doesn't it?

KATHARINA. *(Gives her an unwelcome slap on the back)* Well, you look great! How the hell are you?

PORTIA Why, I'm fine, actually. I say, Katherina, would you be seeking the home of Juliet Capulet, as am I?

KATHARINA. You're darn right – and this is it. I've been here before, you see. I couldn't believe Juliet, of all of us, had the nerve to call this little meeting. Who else is coming – do you know?

7

PORTIA. Not exactly ... we *principal* female characters, of course, but I don't really know who else. I must confess, I *am* surprised to see *you.*

KATHARINA. Oh? Really. Is the old man coming?

PORTIA. The 'old man?' If you mean the Bard, I have no idea. I have come merely to observe the proceedings, and judge the merits of the complaints on a case-by-case basis. I may offer any advice or council that may be of use.

(Enter **NURSE**, *dressed as* **JULIET** *'s* **NURSE** *in contemporary attire, simple housedress and apron.)*

NURSE. Good afternoon, ladies

PORTIA. Good afternoon. This *is* the home of Juliet Capulet?

KATHARINA. *(To* **PORTIA***)* What, you don't believe me?

PORTIA. I didn't mean to imply ...

NURSE. Oh my, my, my, yes this is the home of the Capulets. Please come in. This is Juliet's favorite garden ... God forbid, where is this girl? Now, by my maidenhead, I bade her come *(Calls within)* What, Juliet?

JULIET. *(From within)* I come anon.

NURSE. She'll be joining you shortly. May I get you something to drink?

KATHARINA. Not me.

PORTIA. Not at the moment, thank you. *(She sits and pulls out her cell phone or some papers.)*

NURSE. Then, excuse me while I attend to some details inside.

KATHARINA. Just a moment, don't I know you from somewhere?

NURSE. Well, dearie, I'd wonder if you didn't. Right now, I'm Juliet's nurse, as you know, but you probably remember me as the widow in *your* play.

KATHARINA. The widow ... hmmmm ... the widow?

NURSE. I also have the enormous good fortune to appear as Mistress Quickly in a few of the histories. I take very good care of that rogue Sir John Falstaff.

KATHARINA. Aha! That must be exhausting!

NURSE. Oh, to be sure, to be sure, he is that. Oh! You mean playing all three characters, ma'am. Oh yes, especially at those festivals where they run my shows simultaneously and I have to dash back and forth from scene to scene. Sometimes its just impossible. Well, I must attend to my duties.

KATHARINA. *(Looks after her, then at* PORTIA *– then flounces down into chair next to Portia with a)* Hmmmmmmf!

*(*OPHELIA *enters L twirling and humming to herself, followed by* DESDEMONA.*)*

DESDEMONA. Now, Ophelia, I told you to wait for me, dear.

OPHELIA. *(Stops and hands* DESDEMONA *a stem of Rosemary from the bouquet she is carrying.)* Rosemary – for remembrance. I think you need that, Desdemona.

DESDEMONA. What do you mean, that I'm becoming adlepated, that my mind is failing like yours, young lady?

OPHELIA. Not your mind, Desi, just your memory. You could have avoided a lot of trouble if you remembered where you left your handkerchief. That nasty old Iago would never have been able to accuse you of …

DESDEMONA. Now … now – I was a victim of knavery and malevolence – not of a failing memory, my girl. *(To herself)* Oh, his impossible jealousy – and never did I give him cause.

OPHELIA. You aren't the only victim, Desdemona. It makes me so sad that Hamlet thinks I am as wicked and as black with corruption as his dreadful mother. Poor dear boy, he thinks all women are whores.

DESDEMONA. Ophelia! What can you mean by that?

OPHELIA. He does, he thinks all women act like whores. He overhears my father arranging to use me to discover why Hamlet is behaving so oddly. I know he overhears the conversation and he thinks I am being prostituted, that I have let myself be 'used' by a man. A nunnery, indeed, perhaps that's where I'm headed, I don't know

DESDEMONA. Oh I don't know dear, surely …

OPHELIA. I've tried to be a good girl, a trusted girl, an obedient girl, but I just have to endure all I can endure and at the end, I simply can't take it anymore. *(Starts to sob)*

DESDEMONA. Oh, sweet Ophelia, believe me, not all men think that way about women.

OPHELIA. Desdemona, why is Othello suspicious of you?

DESDEMONA. Ouch! *(She steps back from* **OPHELIA***).*

NURSE. *(Interrupting, appears in doorway with a pitcher of iced tea).* Ladies, welcome. Here is some refreshment for you all. Juliet will be with you anon. Her mother, the lady of the house, and a good lady, and a wise and a virtuous, has her closeted in counsel. I am told to see to your needs.

PORTIA. *(Coming forward)* We are fine, nurse, and thank you.

NURSE. Very well then. Ladies. *(exits)*

PORTIA. *(Coming forward).* Desdemona! How nice to see you. *(Checks out her dress)* Mmm ... lovely fabric. Where are you playing?

DESDEMONA. Missouri Rep, isn't it wonderful? *(the dress)*

PORTIA. And you as well, Ophelia. Are you … well?

OPHELIA. Well, well, well, yes, indeed, very well … all's well that ends well, I suppose, well now, … well? really, yes, well!

DESDEMONA. *(To* **PORTIA***)* You know, she had on a perfectly lovely little yellow silk when I picked her up from the Pasadena production, but she insisted on choosing her own outfit.

OPHELIA. I told you – I'm not playing this weekend, so I dressed myself Tyrone Guthrie *(notes blouse)*, Utah Shakespeare Festival, *(notes skirt)* Wilmington Drama League, *(hat)* and … *(raises skirt to show big black heavy work boots)* … Reed College!!

DESDEMONA. *(Shaking her head at* **OPHELIA** *as* **OPHELIA** *dances off)* Portia, I know why I'm here, but what kind of issues could you possibly have with the old man. You're the heroine, the objective thinker, the wise one, the ... the one with all the great lines!

KATHARINA. *(To herself)* And, she's the one who gets to make fools out of all the male characters!

DESDEMONA. *(Ignoring* KATHARINA.*)* And, you get your man!

KATHARINA. *(Gets up, joins conversation)* And, she gets to make fools out of every single male character! Exactly how many suitors are there, let's see. There's the Neapolitan Prince ...

DESDEMONA. ... who talks of nothing but his horses ...

KATHARINA. ... the county Palatine ...

DESDEMONA. ... such a sad, dour little man ...

KATHARINA. ... the French lord ...

DESDEMONA. ... Oh, now, really!

OPHELIA. *(From the corner)* And, there's Monsieur Le Bon and Faulconbridge ...

DESDEMONA. Falconbridge, oh those clothes! **(OPHELIA** *wanders off)*

DESDEMONA. The Scottish Lord, the Duke of Saxony's nephew ... who else?

PORTIA. Fortune hunters all!! Well, it is true – I am the heroine, and I do get to make fools out of a number of the male characters – but there is just one small element in the plot that disturbs me – and, well, beyond that, I simply want to support my fellow heroines.

(JULIET *enters, smiling)*

JULIET. Ladies, ladies, so sorry I wasn't here when you arrived. I hope you are all comfortable

ALL. *(Mixed thanks, yes, of course, etc.)*

KATHARINA. Oh now, *this* is pretty (JULIET *'s dress)*.

JULIET. Yes, isn't it? Stratford, Ontario.

KATHARINA. Ah, I know the designer ... *very* nice *(nods knowingly)*.

JULIET. Well, hello friends, and welcome to Verona. I hope you are all comfortable.

ALL. Yes, its lovely here, etc.

JULIET. I have noticed, as we have all crossed paths in recent seasons, that we all seem to have 'issues' that concern us about our roles, questions of motivation, and inevitability of plot, and heaven knows what else. So, ladies, I took the liberty of inviting you here to help clear the air. I'm afraid our little meeting is much against the wishes of my father, who, at the very mention of Mr. Shakespeare's name, seems to breathe fire and spew ash from his ears. Papa, as you might expect, has his own very real 'issues' with his character and plot. Mama, however, has given her approval, which I think is very surprising since she always goes along with whatever Papa decides.

DESDEMONA. We've all been dying to know. Will the Bard himself be joining us this afternoon?

JULIET. Oh, dear ladies. I would love to say yes, but it seems he sees very few people these days and he has sent his representative Miss Jacqueline de Boys. I expect that she will be joining us very soon. I've met her and she seems very smart and very kind.

KATHARINA. I knew he wouldn't come!

PORTIA. Now, really, Katharina, I'm sure Ms. De Boys will be most helpful.

*(Enter **OPHELIA** dragging by the hand **JACQUELINE DE BOYS** dressed somewhat "Hollywood" with big sunglasses, scarf, car keys dangling impatiently from her hand).*

OPHELIA. Look what I found in the side garden … just next to that lovely pool of shallow gray water.

DESDEMONA. *(To **OPHELIA**)* Oh you poor sweet girl.

JULIET. Jacqueline – how nice of you to come. You know these ladies, of course – Katharina.

DE BOYS. Kate – *Taming of the Shrew* – we've met *(she ticks her name off in her notebook)*.

KATHARINA. *(Returns her wave with a luke-warm wave-off).*

JULIET. Portia.

DE BOYS. *Merchant of Venice* – nice to see you *(they shake hands).*

JULIET. Desdemona.

DE BOYS. *Othello* – Hello again!

JULIET. And, of course, Ophelia.

OPHELIA. *(Dances around* **DE BOYS***)*

DE BOYS. Yes, *Hamlet.* Of course. Are you expecting anyone else?

JULIET. Actually, Titania said she might flutter in for a bit, but she was having a time of it being at the Laguna Playhouse and a little college theater in Pennsylvania at the same time – she may not make it.

DESDEMONA. Oh, God, I know, sometimes, the schedule is just impossible! Constantly dashing from place to place to be where you're needed. I saw Titania just last week in Oregon.

OPHELIA. What was she wearing?

DESDEMONA. Purple. They've got all the fairies in purple in Ashland this year. She was terribly busy, though, poor thing.

KATHARINA. Yes, she is just *so* popular, as always. I just closed at the Public in New York, and they're having her back again next season.

PORTIA. Really?

KATHARINA. *(On her soapbox)* I just don't get it. It's always the fairies, fairies, fairies. How about poor Hermia? She loves Lysander and her father wants to put her to death since she doesn't want to marry her father's pal Demetrius. Death!! … that's not kidding around. People always miss the point. She is going to die or get sent to a nunnery by the Duke for life. She just wants a little control over her own life. That's why they run to the forest. But, oh, no. The fairies always get the big marketing hype.

DE BOYS. Well, well, I see there are definitely some issues to be discussed. I think we'd better get started – so who is first?

JULIET. Well, Jackie, *(serving drinks)* I'd really like to point out that we didn't mean to call you here just to attack you personally. We know you are only Will's publisher.

DE BOYS. AND literary agent!

JULIET. And agent, of course. We hope you understand that there are just a few … issues … regarding some of our plots which might make our lives a little easier if they were, should I say "fixed," that is to say …

KATHARINA. *(Rolling over her line)* Maybe, after all these years, its time to do a little update . .

PORTIA. *(Interrupting)* Heaven knows, some of us have very little to complain of, to be sure!

JULIET. But I, for instance, still fail to understand why I can't simply wake up – just at that last moment, that almost final moment, the moment that everyone, the entire audience, night after night, I must say, is waiting for with baited breath, just before my Romeo drinks HIS poison. Then, he wouldn't have to die, and I wouldn't have to stab myself – which is really rather a nuisance every performance.

OPHELIA. *(Gathers together* **DESDEMONA** *and* **JULIET***)* Yes, I should say so. And what about us?

DE BOYS. I'm sorry?

OPHELIA. Us, the dead girls *(the three join arms around each other)* …DROWNED! *(referring to herself)*

DESDEMONA. … SMOTHERED …

JULIET. … STABBED!

OPHELIA. I'm sorry, I know we all have legitimate complaints, but it's a whole different story when you have to die every single show.

DESDEMONA. Yes, the 'stabbed, smothered and drowned girls' … maybe somebody will write a ballad for us. Might make a catchy tune.

(Insert Song – optional – to the tune of old Irish ballad
Ode to Whiskey – JULIET, DESDEMONA & OPHELIA.
See page 24 for music.)

ALL. To say that we're puppets of men's ideas
　　An argument can be found.
　　But how can we argue for what we believe
　　When we're

JULIET. stabbed,

DESDEMONA.　　smothered

OPHELIA.　　　　　and drowned.

ALL. Could it be just a matter of course,
　　When we're never allowed to feel remorse,
　　But how can we challenge our Bard's renown,
　　When we're

JULIET. stabbed,

DESDEMONA.　　smothered

OPHELIA.　　　　　and drowned.

ALL. Living happily a – a – after
　　Is not in the cards for we ladies fair
　　For that would our plots forever confound
　　Since we're

JULIET. stabbed,

DESDEMONA.　　smothered

OPHELIA.　　　　　and drowned.

(Fourth, fifth and sixth verse are dance choreography
and humming, each verse ending)

ALL. We've been

JULIET. stabbed

DESDEMONA.　　smothered

OPHELIA.　　　　　and drowned

ALL. Always

JULIET. stabbed

DESDEMONA.　　smothered

OPHELIA.   and drowned

DE BOYS. Well that was lovely, but excuse me if I'm trying to keep this straight – So *you*, Juliet, wouldn't actually die, is that it?

OPHELIA. *(To* **DE BOYS***)* It would rather destabilize the storyline, wouldn't it?

DESDEMONA. I think, Jackie, all she is asking for is perhaps a happy ending. Heaven knows …

DE BOYS. *(Interrupting)* Now hold on – there IS a happy ending – The Montagues and Capulets reconcile over Romeo and Juliet's dead bodies. Isn't that good enough? *(Aside)* Oh, he's going to love this one.

JULIET. Why couldn't they reconcile over my ATTEMPTED suicide – like the friar intended? Just to scare them. To prove I'd rather die than marry that putrid Paris.

DE BOYS. But that would mean …

OPHELIA. I think it's a lovely idea. Just as I think it would be a lovely idea if Hamlet could just for a moment reveal his true feelings to me – instead of driving me absolutely *insane* with confusion!

DE BOYS. It just doesn't work, though, does it. What sends you over the edge in this tragedy is the combination of your mutual unfulfilled love and the fact that Hamlet kills your father. I mean, that's really the biggie, isn't it?

OPHELIA. It would just be *nice*, that's all I'm saying.

DE BOYS. Nice! Did I hear the word nice? So let me get this straight – you want everybody to live happily ever after, is that it?

DESDEMONA. Is there … is there something wrong with that?

OPHELIA. Well, is there?

KATHARINA. It works for me!

DE BOYS. *(Explodes)* Except that *Romeo and Juliet* is *a TRAGEDY!*

KATHARINA. *(Goes after* **DE BOYS***, jabbing her arm and pushing her back with every statement)* Do you want to see a tragedy? I'll show you a tragedy. *I'm* a tragedy! Being humiliated by your intended husband at every turn – that's a tragedy. Being kept waiting at the altar – that's a tragedy. Dragging through muck and mire in your wedding dress – that's a tragedy.

ALL. *(Little snickers and laughter).*

PORTIA. *(She makes several attempts to control her laughter during this speech).* I know it may not seem quite rational to you, especially when it was performed today, in twenty-first century. Especially since its not very politically correct, and even, I admit, very humiliating in some ways, but, I don't know if you have much of a case there, Katherina – it really is all very funny!

KATHARINA. Well! I thought this would be the ONE place I would get some support, *sisters. (Moves off in a huff,* OPHELIA *comforts her).*

DESDEMONA. But, Katharina, yours is only *one* of the issues we're discussing. I need to ask ... amid the unrelenting betrayal in my story, why, in heaven's name, am I undone by having misplaced my handkerchief of all things. My wonderful Othello can't be that stupid, can he? Even Ophelia can't quite comprehend that action. I mean, you know, just read the reviews – over the past four hundred years – I've been described as the 'gentle Desdemona', the 'true and loving wife' of Othello, a 'maiden never bold, the sweetest innocent that ever did lift up eye' – and yet, others say that I am courageous and of unusual intelligence and imagination – to marry the Moor, a radical decision against all custom and tradition. Now, I ask you, am I a complete idiot ... or an inspiring heroine?

DE BOYS. I believe "he" might refer to you as "complicated."

PORTIA. Strong, rational, complicated women are, I am afraid few in any of our plays.

JULIET. You may be a little sensitive on that point, Portia.

DE BOYS. *(To* PORTIA*)* And I don't agree with you at all. And

I know "he" wouldn't agree. There's Cleopatra.

KATHARINA. And Lady *(shudder)* Mac Beth.

OPHELIA. And Gertrude, my own Hamlet's mother.

PORTIA. I did say 'rational.'

KATHARINA. What a crew – strong women or sleepwalking homicidal maniacs all.

DESDEMONA. Yes, quite a collection of womanhood. All role models, surely.

DE BOYS. What about Katharina's example of Hermia in *Midsummer Night's Dream,* she's strong, courageous AND romantic. She has the courage to run away when her own father threatened her with death, rather than marry her father's choice – a man whom she doesn't love.

JULIET. Yes, she is my hero.

DE BOYS. And Rosalind in *As You Like It.* There's courage, and strength *and* determination.

KATHARINA. But she had to dress like a boy to accomplish her goals.

ALL. *(General mumbling, Yes, how about that?, etc.)*

PORTIA. Well I certainly am familiar with that tactic.

DE BOYS Yes, its true, Rosalind does dress like a boy and then 'disappears' from the knowledge of her lover, but the entire audience knows that under the doublet beats the heart of the heroine.

KATHARINA. Oh, give me a break!

PORTIA. Sounds familiar. If you want to have the freedom to speak in a male-dominated world, sometimes you have to dress as a man, or at least adopt the attitude that putting on men's clothes gives you.

KATHARINA. What do you mean? Your attitude changes?

PORTIA. I've talked to the other pants-role girls many times and its universal. Your voice changes, your walk … you kind of swagger just a bit …and you actually feel taller. Its very interesting.

JULIET. I believe we may be getting a little off the target, ladies.

DE BOYS. Yes, I think so too. If I may, I believe I can make a summation of sorts.

JULIET. Do, please go ahead.

DE BOYS. We have female characters from three tragedies and two comedies with "issues" about their plots. Now I'm trying to follow this, but it seems that the characters in the comedies think their shows should be tragedies and the characters in the tragedies believe they should have happy endings, which might not exactly make them comedies – but would seriously affect their dramatic content.

PORTIA. Objection!

DE BOYS. I beg your pardon, Portia?

PORTIA. I hadn't planned to bring up any of my own issues, but I suppose I should make it quite clear that I have a problem with "Merchant" being classified *as* a comedy. Yes, there are many funny bits – but ask Shylock if it is a comedy and you will get another answer – when all his worldly goods are forfeit and this devout Jewish gentlemen is forced against his will to become a Christian. It certainly is a tragedy for old Shylock. That's why I was surprised to see Katharina when we arrived. One "true" comedy" among these outright tragedies.

KATHARINA. I claim the plot of "Shrew" is a tragedy, of sorts – it is for me at any rate – to be humiliated into submission. Is there something funny about that?

JULIET. *(Goes to her consolingly)* And then loved beyond all understanding for the remainder of her days, dowry aside.

KATHARINA. Well, there *is* that. But do the means justify the end? … I've always wondered … what kind of message does that send to all the women who followed us? We've had four centuries of being belittled, betrayed and bullied and I think we've had enough!

DE BOYS. In many ways I agree with you. Do you have any idea what a marketing nightmare producing Shrew represents these days?? But, kidding aside, I don't mean to trivialize your thoughts. What about your final speech in the play, the longest in the script, I might add? Frothing over with obedience and duty, chastising other women for their shrewish behavior. Let's hear some of that to remind us, Katharina.

KATHARINA. *Thy husband is thy lord, thy life, thy keeper,*
Thy head, thy sovereign;

ALL. *(Groans, ad libs, etc.)*

KATHARINA. *(continues) ... one that cares for thee,*
And for thy maintenance commits his body
To painful labor both by sea and land,
To watch the night in storms, the day in cold,
Whilst thou liest warm at home, secure and safe,
And craves no other tribute at thy hands
But love, fair looks and true obedience;

ALL. *(ad lib Now really, good grief, etc.)*

KATHARINA. *(Finishes) Too little payment for so great a debt."*

DE BOYS. Now wait a minute, girls, surely you can hear the sarcasm, the mocking glee she takes in ruffling Petruchio's feathers. Go on, Katharina, don't mind them.

KATHARINA. *I am ashamed that women are so simple*
To offer war where they should kneel for peace;
Or seek for rule, supremacy and sway,
When they are bound to serve, love and obey.

PORTIA. Jackie, is there a reason you're torturing us like this?

DE BOYS. *(Rising impatience)* Yes, can't you hear it? Mr. S. was making a huge statement about men's inflexibility and women's adaptability. And in the end, Katharina keeps her own kind of control. Juliet, what is that final line of Lucentio's which closes the play?

JULIET. "'Tis a wonder, she will be tamed so.!"

DE BOYS. She hasn't been 'tamed' at all! She's just grown up and decided to choose her battles in her world.

KATHARINA. Very few of my actresses play her that way.

DE BOYS. Speak to them. Suggest it. You are the timeless essence of your character. Whisper your thoughts to them. They all need guidance.

KATHARINA. I will. Thank you.

OPHELIA. *(Has been standing to the rear with her back to the audience, begins in this position, and* **ALL** *move away as she begins to speak.)* It seems to me, and I do still have the occasional lucid moment, that our dear Bard expects us all to make sacrifices of some kind – that is, for the purpose of the story, of course.

DE BOYS. Thank you, Ophelia! Well, what do you *all* think *is* the purpose of his plays?

JULIET. To be amusing, to make us laugh?

DE BOYS. That's one.

OPHELIA. To teach.

DE BOYS. To teach what?

DESDEMONA. To teach us, to teach us about ourselves.

KATHARINA. About power and control!

PORTIA. About greed and injustice.

DESDEMONA. About the irony of misthought actions.

OPHELIA. And the tragic consequences of jealousy.

JULIET. About just being human.

(General agreement after each offering.)

DE BOYS. So what you're left with is that, in order to teach these things, which you all feel are important *(general agreement, oh yes, most definitely, etc.)*, you all have some sort of sacrifice to make, as Ophelia so aptly stated. You know, we are the person that we are *because* of our experience, be those experiences good or not very good. They make us who we are. Let us take one character at a time as an example. *(To* **KATHARINA***)* You would like to eliminate from your plot your painful experiences, some disgraceful episodes, some mortifying circumstances.

KATHARINA. I wouldn't miss the muck and the mire.

DE BOYS. But, would you be willing to go back to the sate of inexperience and ignorance you were in before these things happened?

KATHARINA. Oh good grief, you're getting awfully philosophical. *(Pause.)* Well, I really was quite a "shrew" ... and I am much happier now. *(Shakes her head in resignation)*

OPHELIA. Katharina, I'm afraid this is a *very* surreal conversation.

KATHARINA. Well, how about you, Ophelia, what if you were to go back to *your* old state, do you think you would be likely to commit the same folly over again?

OPHELIA. Sadly, I'm afraid I would.

PORTIA. *(Shaking her head.)* Tsk Tsk.

OPHELIA. *(To* **PORTIA***)* Now, Portia, don't be smug. How many of us would be willing to completely wipe out our experiences? They're part of our character, and it would be taking away a portion of our nature. Speak to Shylock about this at some point.

PORTIA. I will.

JULIET. *(Sighs)* Is it just me? I'm afraid sometimes I just get so confused – with the secondary plots, the sub-plots, the side-plots, and the parallel plots.

ALL. *(General agreement)*

DE BOYS. But the plots have their roots in the experience of the characters!

NURSE. *(Enters and observes discussion)*

DESDEMONA. *(To* **DE BOYS***)* So what you're saying is that If we were to part with experiences gained, even through pain, we would first part with one bit of ourselves, and then with another, until at last we would have nothing left except the shell of our former self.

KATHARINA. I'm sure Titania would most definitely be grateful to escape falling in love with a donkey in every performance, but listen girls, it's our responsibility after all to …

NURSE. Milady, if I may, I have been listening to your complaints, or that is "issues," this whole afternoon, and I really must speak.

JULIET. By all means, sweet nurse.

NURSE. By my troth, miladies, be yourselves! Be you. Generations, I should say, centuries of ladies have felt what you all have felt, have looked up to you, cried with you, been angry with you, and left the theater realizing something about themselves which you helped them discover.

JULIET. Nurse?

DE BOYS. She's right. There were two feuding families in Boston in 1822 and by some chance they were both at a showing of Romeo and Juliet on the same evening and they ended their feud so that their young people could be happy.

DE BOYS And surely you all remember how that fellow Leonard Bernstein took Juliet's great love and turned it into *West Side Story*. That woke a lot of people up in the same way in the twentieth century.

OPHELIA. *(Wraps a scarf around her head and sings, dancing around Katharina's chair)* Suddenly I feel pretty, oh so pretty!

KATHARINA. Ophelia! Sit!

OPHELIA. Yes, ma'am.

JULIET. Go ahead, nurse.

NURSE. *(To DESDEMONA)* A woman saw *Othello* in Toronto in 1953 and swore an end to her relationship with a jealous and angry man.

DESDEMONA. *(Jumping up and shouting)* YES! *(Looks around)* Oh, sorry.

NURSE. One young cantankerous woman in Denver in 1892 watched *Shrew* and decided that to get the love she wanted and needed so desperately, that she needed to become lovable. *(To KATHARINA)* No offence, ma'am.

KATHARINA. None taken, as long as you swear not to

mention that silly Cole Porter musical *Kiss Me Kate*. My story may be a farce, but a musical? I don't think so.

ALL. (*General laughter*)

NURSE. The list goes on and on over the four centuries – all over the planet – you ladies know the stories. Don't water it down to make it more palatable and fashionable for today's audiences. Mr. S. may have made our lives a little difficult at times, but you know he sees right into our hearts and shows us our whole societies' strengths and failings.

JULIET. Well I think that maybe we're all just exhausted.

DE BOYS. And so you should be Its exhausting work. But its your job.

DESDEMONA. Indeed. Every new generation needs to be reminded how far women have come since the self-destructive patriarchy of the sixteenth century.

PORTIA. Well said, Desdemona.

OPHELIA. Shakespeare's women – all of us – break stereotypes about women's influence in a man's world.

PORTIA. Let's face it, some of us are able to solve problems that male characters can't fix, in ways they would never dream of.

DE BOYS. (*To* **JULIET**) Just knowing that should make you just a little less exhausted.

JULIET. Yes, of course it does. Well said, gentle nurse. Thank you for adding your insights.

ALL. (*Light applause.*)

NURSE. Now, ladies, I have some nice chilled dill cucumber soup, some roasted chicken with sage, some green tomatoes in a roasted garlic vinaigrette, and a bottle of bubbly wine the monks gave me – all ready for our lunch – come go on in and we'll all toast our friend Will. Come along, now, that way, there you go!

(*Exit* **ALL** *but* **NURSE** *and* **J. DE BOYS.**)

NURSE. (*To* **DE BOYS**) Well, your Mr. S. owes me one now, don't you think?

DE BOYS. What did you have in mind?

NURSE. Let's see, some day I'd like to have a nice sit-down and see if the "Widow" in Shrew might have just a few more lines, so that somebody might remember her *(Going off)*. And, about that Falstaff …

DE BOYS. Falstaff? Oh now, must we? We're about to eat!

(They exit)

(Drop Lights)

(OPTIONAL ENDING: All but the nurse exit to the house for lunch. Shakespeare enters from garden.

NURSE. *Well, Mr. S. I believe you owe me one, now, don't you think?*

SHAKESPEARE. *What is it now?*

NURSE. *Don't you think the widow in Shrew might have just a few more lines, so somebody remembers her?*

SHAKESPEARE. *I can look at it.*

NURSE. *And about that Falstaff …*

SHAKESPEARE. *You're not going to start nagging me about Falstaff again, are you? Really, now, I'm starving, let's just go have lunch.)*

Stabbed, Smothered and Drowned

Lyrics by Judy Elliot McDonald
Adapted from the melody "Ode To Whiskey" by Turlough O'Carolan

Arranged by Lowell E. Kobrin

To say that we're pup - pets of men's i - deas an ar - gu-ment can be found.___ But how can we ar-gue for what we be-lieve when we're stabbed___ smo-thered and drowned. Could it be just a matter of course when we're ne-ver al - lowed to feel re-morse. But how can we chal-lenge our Bard's re-known when we're stabbed___ smo-thered and drowned. Liv___ing hap-pily af___ ter___ is not in the cards for we la-dies fair. For that would our plots for ever con-found since we're stabbed___ smo-thered and drowned.

COSTUME PLOT

PORTIA
Hip, contemporary successful business suit, heels, leather brief-case and cell phone. Looks like a New York or San Francisco corporate attorney.

KATHARINA
Renaissance upper-class wedding dress in colors of red and gold. With embroidered bodice, two layers of skirts, etc. Jewelry includes necklace, circlet, rings.

NURSE
Contemporary warm-weather housedress, apron, sandals.

DESDEMONA
Flowing medieval dress in soft dark colors, dark blue, burgundy, etc. Split over-sleeves, full skirt, perhaps even a small train. Very flowing.

OPHELIA
A total mess. Bizarre mix of Shakespearean and contemporary clothing with hat and bodice, badly mismatched. Must have big, heavy black combat boots.

JULIET
Sweet, lovely traditional 15th century gown in pale pink or beige, very soft, circlet and necklace, matching sandals.

JACQUELINE DE BOYS
'L.A.' business clothes. Short skirt, suit jacket, heels, scarf, lots of jewelry and sunglasses, carrying rattling car keys.

(OPTIONAL) SHAKESPEARE
Tights, balloon pants and coat, dark color, white collar.

PROPERTIES

Usable cell phone for Portia. Must ring in audience.
Briefcase with paperwork for Portia.
Small 'bouquet' of twigs and greens for Ophelia.
Notebook, pen and briefcase of planner for J. DeBoys.
Pitcher of iced tea and tea towel for Nurse.
Preset: Tray and six goblets/glasses.

SOUNDSCAPE

Birdsong :30 - :60 fade at :30. For opening and repeat at end.
Music (sheet music included) or use royalty-free download of 'Ode
to Whiskey,' 17th century ditty attributed to Turlogh O'Carolan.

OTHER TITLES AVAILABLE FROM SAMUEL FRENCH

MUSIC FROM DOWN THE HILL
John Ford Noonan

Drama / 2f / Interior

The setting is a psychiatric clinic atop a hill in the beautiful country town of Woodstock, New York. Claire Granick, a young schizophrenic who loves Bruce Springsteen to death and cannot for the life of her tell the truth, regularly drives out new roommates with terror tactics and Springsteen songs played too loud. Enter Margot Yossarian, a middle aged hysteric with a huge heart and a frightened body who also loves rock n roll, especially the music of the 60s: Hendrix, Joplin, The Doors, Cream. Claire's usually effective tactics don't undermine Margot, but rather release her stiffened body and send her to a soaring state of health dreamed of but never expected by the head of the hospital. In Act II, Margot attempts to help Claire break through her problems. Is she successful? Is rock n roll truly deep and loud enough to heal the mentally disturbed? Can the concept of rock penetrate the disturbed heart and create a miracle of mental health? Do people this disturbed ever successfully get back to the outside?

"A delicacy of feeling that is rare in theatre pieces today.... A cannily constructed melange of alienation [and] nostalgia..."
– *The New York Times*

www.ingramcontent.com/pod-product-compliance
Lightning Source LLC
Chambersburg PA
CBHW070404120726
47909CB00008B/2990